Family Day

by Eileen Kurtis-Kleinman
illustrated by Jessica Schiffman

Orlando   Boston   Dallas   Chicago   San Diego

Visit *The Learning Site!*

www.harcourtschool.com

This is my family. I have a grandmother and a grandfather. I have a mother and a father. I have a brother and a baby sister.

There are lots more people in the Lanza family. We will see them all at the Lanza Family Reunion.

I have lots of aunts and uncles and plenty of cousins, too. Once a year all the people in the Lanza family get together. We meet at my grandpa's and grandma's house in the country.

The first person I see is my Aunt Tina. I call her Aunt Tina because she is married to Uncle Vanni. Uncle Vanni is my father's brother. Aunt Tina gives me a great big hug. She tells me I am her favorite niece.

Aunt Tina and Uncle Vanni have a daughter. She is eight years old, just like me. Her name is Mirella. She is my cousin and I am her cousin. Cousin Mirella and I have a plan. We sneak up to the attic.

My grandparents have lived in this
house for fifty years. There are
wonderful treasures in the attic! I find
my grandmother's hat. Mirella finds
her father's baseball mitt and a very
old baby stroller.

My little brother, Fredo, finds us in the attic. He wants to know what we are doing. We decide to tell him about our plan.

Cousin Mirella and I try to plan our surprise. We are just starting to practice when we hear a shout from downstairs.

"Hello cousins! What are you doing up there?" my father calls up to us.

My brother Fredo, my cousin Mirella, and I all climb down the stairs.

"Please help your grandmother in the kitchen," my father says to us. "She wants to teach her grandson and her granddaughters her secret recipe."

The kitchen is a very busy place.
Grandma Lanza is cooking sauce. My
mother is feeding my baby sister,
Sandra.

"Is it time for the surprise yet?" my
brother Fredo asks.

"Not yet," I say.

Grandpa Lanza is in the garden. Fredo is helping him pick tomatoes for the salad.

"Thank you, grandson," Grandpa Lanza says to Fredo. "You have grown as tall as a tree!"

Everyone sits down at the long tables. Uncle Vanni sits down next to Fredo.

"Hello, nephew," he says to Fredo. "It's time to eat!"

"There's going to be a surprise after dinner," whispers Fredo.

The food is so good! While everyone is eating, Mirella and I try to count the family. We have two grandparents, five aunts, three uncles, and seven cousins.

Then it's time for our surprise. We put on old clothes. Mirella and I start to sing. Fredo tries to play the trumpet. Grandfather Lanza laughs. Grandmother Lanza smiles. Father taps his foot. Mother claps her hands.

Uncle Vanni gets his guitar and plays an old song that Grandpa and Grandma know. Then all the cousins hold hands in a circle. Grandpa and Grandma dance together in the middle. Everyone cheers!

Grandpa and Grandma Lanza are
very happy. Our family had a
wonderful time together. Now it is
time to say good-bye. See you again
next year!